ALI BABA BERNSTEIN,
LOST AND FOUND

ALI BABA BERNSTEIN,
LOST AND FOUND

BY
JOHANNA HURWITZ

ILLUSTRATED
BY KAREN MILONE

Morrow Junior Books
New York

For a good friend,
lost and found:
Cecile Saretsky

Printed in the United States of America.
1   2   3   4   5   6   7   8   9   10

Library of Congress Cataloging-in-Publication Data
Hurwitz, Johanna.
Ali Baba Bernstein, lost and found / Johanna Hurwitz; illustrated
by Karen Milone.
p.   cm.
Summary: Throughout a series of adventures, ten-year-old David
"Ali Baba" Bernstein spends most of his time thinking about becoming
a detective and getting a dog.
ISBN 0-688-11454-7 (trade)—0-688-11455-5 (library)
[1. Detectives—Fiction.   2. New York (N.Y.)—Fiction.   3. Humorous stories.]
I. Milone-Dugan, Karen, ill.   II. Title.
PZ7.H9574At   1992
[Fic]—dc20   92-4774   CIP   AC

CONTENTS

1. ALI BABA AND THE CASE OF THE MYSTERIOUS BAG

David Bernstein was not like most of the other boys in his class at school. In the first place, back when he was only eight years, five months, and seventeen days old, he had given himself a new name. David Bernstein insisted that he wanted to be known as Ali Baba. That way he would not be confused with the three other boys named David in his class. And as Ali Baba, strange and mysterious things were sure to happen to him.

1

At home, he was the only David in his family. But even though they had no confusion about his identity, his parents, like his teachers, gradually found themselves calling him by his new name.

There was another way in which Ali Baba Bernstein differed from boys his age. Though he watched baseball, football, basketball, and hockey games on television, he was not crazy about sports. Though he accumulated stamps and baseball cards and superhero comic books, he was not a dedicated collector. By the time Ali Baba Bernstein was nine years, eleven months, and five days old, he was devoting most of his energy to developing his skills as a detective. He watched for suspicious people and occurrences. So far he hadn't found too many cases waiting to be solved. Still, he wanted to be ready when the time came.

Lately, Ali Baba had been thinking about getting a dog. A bloodhound would be a very useful pet for a boy who wanted to be a detective.

"A bloodhound?" gasped Mrs. Bernstein when Ali Baba first suggested it. "Do you know how big a bloodhound is?"

"Then how about a German shepherd?" suggested Ali Baba. He had seen a program on television that showed these dogs sniffing for drugs and explosives at airports. A German shepherd would be a pretty neat pet, too, he thought.

"This apartment isn't big enough for those big dogs," his mother said. "Besides, it's a lot of work having a dog in a New York City apartment. I don't think you're ready for such a responsibility."

"How about a smaller dog?" asked Ali Baba. Surely a smaller dog would be a smaller responsibility.

"No dogs," said his mother, shaking her head.

"We'll talk about it another time, when you're older," said his father, holding out a slim hope for the future.

Ali Baba was already nine years, eleven months, and five days old. He wondered how much older he would have to be to convince his parents that he was old enough to take responsibility for a dog. He'd have to work hard to show them that he wasn't still a little kid.

On the Sunday afternoon that Ali Baba was

nine years, eleven months, and eleven days old, he went to the movies with his best friend, Roger Zucker. The movie theater was just across the street from Roger's apartment building, and they were showing two old James Bond movies. James Bond was a secret agent who could never be tricked. Ali Baba had seen all of the James Bond movies. He practically knew them by heart. Still, he enjoyed watching them over and over so that he could learn from them. He did not want to be tricked when he became a secret agent someday.

Ali Baba and Roger settled into their seats. Just before the first movie began, a very tall man came down the aisle and sat right in front of Ali Baba.

"Darn," complained Ali Baba. "Now I can't see."

"I'll move over," offered Roger. He slid down one seat, and Ali Baba sat in Roger's old one.

Now Ali Baba could see without any problem. The lights dimmed and the first film began. Although he watched the movie with interest, from time to time Ali Baba found himself looking at the profile of the tall man

4

in the row ahead. His jaw was going up and down because he was chewing gum. This was a little strange. Not many of the grown-ups Ali Baba knew chewed gum. Mostly, kids did.

Ali Baba noticed a bag under the man's seat. It was a brown paper bag, the kind they used when you bought groceries at the store. Ali Baba wondered what the man had in his bag. Perhaps he had brought a snack to eat at the movies. Something exciting happened on the screen, and Ali Baba turned his attention back to the film. The next time he looked in the man's direction, the seat was empty. He must have gone to get some popcorn, Ali Baba decided. When the first film ended, the man had not returned.

Ali Baba turned around to check if the man had changed his seat. It was difficult to see well in the dark, but the man had been so tall that Ali Baba didn't think he could miss him. Then he had another thought. He bent down and looked under the seat where the man had been sitting. The paper bag was still there.

Ali Baba felt a shiver go down his spine. He grabbed Roger by the arm. "I think there's a bomb under there," he said, pointing to the empty seat in front of them.

"You're crazy," said Roger. "Why would someone put a bomb in this movie theater?"

"Why not?" asked Ali Baba.

"You don't even know what a bomb looks like," said Roger.

"Yes, I do," whispered Ali Baba. "They're round and heavy, sort of like a bowling ball," he said with authority. He had seen bombs dropping from airplanes in old movies about World War II on television.

"We better get out of here," he said to Roger. "That bomb might explode any moment." He slid off his seat and tried pulling Roger along by the arm.

"Listen, I want to see the second movie," Roger protested.

"How can you see a movie if this theater blows up?" Ali Baba argued. "Come on. Hurry!"

"That bag is probably empty," grumbled Roger, remaining seated.

Ali Baba was nervous about touching the bag, but he knew he had to investigate the situation. He moved the bag gently with the tip of his sneaker. "There's something in there, all right," he said.

"It must be garbage. You know, candy

wrappers and an empty soda cup. Stuff like that."

"No," said Ali Baba. "It feels too heavy." He wanted to open the bag, but he was afraid of setting off the bomb inside. "That man put a bomb under the seat, and then he left the movie theater. We could all blow up at any time."

"Will you kids please shut up?" said a man sitting behind them. "How can anyone watch a movie with you making so much noise?"

"Forget it," whispered Roger to Ali Baba. The second movie had begun, and he turned his attention back to the screen.

Ali Baba could not possibly forget a bomb under the seat in front of him. He would never forgive himself if the theater blew up and everyone in it was killed. He bent down and gingerly sniffed at the paper bag. It had a slightly sweet odor that was vaguely familiar. He wondered what the trained dogs smelled when they were detecting bombs. Ali Baba picked up the paper bag very gently. He did not want to shake the bomb and set it off. It was heavy. He felt the paper and his fingers made out a round shape inside.

"It is a bomb. I knew it," gasped Ali Baba.

He could feel the hairs on his arms rise up with the scary thrill of holding a bag with a bomb inside it. Even as he worried about the danger, he could imagine the newspaper headline: BRAVE BOY SAVES LIVES OF HUNDREDS IN MOVIE THEATER. It would certainly convince his parents that he had a sense of responsibility. You couldn't be more responsible than that—risking your life to save others. Maybe the mayor would award him with a medal for bravery. And his parents would let him get a dog.

With one hand, Ali Baba held on to the bag. With the other, he grabbed Roger. "Come on. Let's get this thing out of here," he hissed. "We may have waited too long already." He yanked Roger's arm really hard. Then Ali Baba ran up the aisle, with Roger following reluctantly behind him.

He ran out to the lobby where there was enough light to see what the bomb looked like. Ali Baba carefully opened the paper bag and, sure enough, inside was a heavy, round object. However, it wasn't black the way the bombs were in the movies. It was more of a tan color and had stripes down its sides. Although he had never seen a bomb like this before, Ali Baba thought it looked amazingly familiar.

He didn't see a fuse on it, but he still worried that it might explode right in his hands. He needed a minute to think.

"You hold it," he said, tossing the bomb to the man who had collected tickets from them earlier.

"What do I want this for?" asked the man. He tossed the round object back to Ali Baba.

"I found this bomb inside," said Ali Baba, juggling the thing in his hands. "I don't know what to do with it." The headline in his imagination was changing to BOY EXPLODES WHILE HOLDING BOMB IN LOBBY OF MOVIE THEATER. He tossed the bomb back to the ticket collector.

"Bomb?" gasped the ticket collector as he caught the object a second time. He immediately threw it back to Ali Baba.

"Yes. It was hidden under the seat in front of me," said Ali Baba. "It may have a timing device inside it. We've got to get it to the police."

"Stop pulling my leg," said the ticket collector. He grabbed the round ball from Ali Baba.

"Be careful," shouted Ali Baba, jumping away.

The ticket collector inspected what he was holding.

"I don't think it really is a bomb," said Roger. "It looks an awful lot like a cantaloupe to me."

"A cantaloupe?" asked Ali Baba.

"Yes. A cantaloupe," said the ticket collector.

No wonder it looked familiar. Ali Baba felt himself blushing with embarrassment. How could he have been so stupid?

"I really should throw you kids out of here," complained the ticket collector. "I don't have time for April Fools' jokes, especially when it isn't the first of April."

"Let's go see the rest of the movie," said Roger. "We'll be very good," he promised the man.

Ali Baba followed his friend back into the dark theater. There were no newspaper headlines in his imagination now, just an awful sense of embarrassment. However, as he sat down once again, it occurred to him that someone could disguise a bomb to look and smell exactly like a cantaloupe. It was the sort of thing that could happen in a James Bond movie any day. Ali Baba sighed. It just wasn't the sort of thing that happened in his life. How could he prove he was responsible if he never had the opportunity? Ali Baba wondered if the ticket collector was going to take the cantaloupe home to eat. By rights, thought Ali Baba, it belongs to me. After all, finders keepers.

But whoever ate the cantaloupe, there was still an unsolved mystery for Ali Baba to ponder: Why would someone bring a cantaloupe to the movies?

2. ALI BABA HUNTS FOR A BEAR

*T*he summer after Ali Baba's tenth birthday, he and his parents went on a trip to Wyoming. When Mr. Bernstein first announced to his son that they were going to vacation in a couple of parks, Ali Baba thought he was making a joke.

The Bernsteins' apartment in New York City was near two parks—Riverside Park and Central Park. Both were nice places. When he was little, Ali Baba had played in the sandbox

13

or on the swings and slides in the parks. It was good to have trees and grass in the middle of the city. But how could you take a vacation in the park?

"These parks are different," Mr. Bernstein explained to his son. "National parks are huge, and people come from all over the country to visit them."

"People come from all over the world," Ali Baba's mother added.

Ali Baba was sure they were exaggerating.

On the day that Ali Baba Bernstein was ten years, two months, and seven days old, they arrived in Grand Teton National Park in Wyoming. Then he saw that his parents had not been exaggerating at all. The park was huge. In fact, it looked bigger than Riverside Park and Central Park and a hundred other parks combined. And just as his parents had said, it was filled with thousands and thousands of tourists.

Some were Americans like Ali Baba. He began noticing the license plates on the cars. In the first hour in the park, he spotted plates from Illinois, Colorado, California, and Wyoming. The car that Mr. Bernstein had rented had license plates from Minnesota. When they stopped for lunch, a man came over to them.

"Whereabouts in Minnesota do you live?" he asked.

"We live in New York," said Mr. Bernstein, explaining about the rented car.

"I was born in St. Paul, Minnesota," said the man. "I thought you might come from there, too."

Ali Baba and his parents were staying in a little log cabin. In the parking lot near the cabins, there were three huge buses. The men and women coming out of the buses looked just like Americans, but Ali Baba couldn't understand a single word they said.

"What are they saying?" he asked his parents.

"I don't know," said Mrs. Bernstein. "They are speaking German." Because she didn't know the language, she could only guess what the people were talking about.

What most people seemed to be talking about were the animals. The park was filled with them. At home, the only animals Ali Baba ever saw in the park were squirrels and dogs. The dogs were supposed to be kept on leashes, but they often ran loose.

Here, there were herds of buffalo and antelope and deer. Sometimes you could see them very close to the road. Other times they were off in the distance.

Mr. Bernstein had brought a pair of binoculars, and Ali Baba kept busy searching for animals. He thought he would ask his father if he could borrow the binoculars when he got home. They seemed like very useful equipment for a would-be detective.

"I saw a bear," a girl told Ali Baba proudly as he was adjusting the binoculars at a lookout point the first morning.

"Where?" asked Ali Baba. He wondered if the girl was telling the truth. He hadn't seen any bears.

"Not here," said the girl. "When we were driving in Yellowstone National Park."

"Was it big?" asked Ali Baba.

"Huge," said the girl.

It seemed as if everything in the park was huge.

"Maybe I'll see a bear, too," said Ali Baba, putting the binoculars to his eyes.

"You probably won't," said the girl. "It's very hard to see them nowadays. My father

16

said that when he came here twenty years ago, there were lots of bears."

"If you saw one, then I'll see one," said Ali Baba with certainty. He was determined to see a bear before he went back to New York City.

After that, Ali Baba spent all his time searching for a bear.

Mr. Bernstein took loads of pictures. He made Ali Baba smile into the camera at least a dozen times a day. Ali Baba found that very boring. It was embarrassing, too, if there were other people around. Most of the time, however, the other people were so busy posing and taking their own pictures that they didn't even notice.

"I see a bear!" Ali Baba shouted that afternoon.

"Where? Where?" asked his mother, looking around.

Mr. Bernstein grabbed his camera, ready to focus it at the elusive animal.

"Ha-ha! I made you look!" Ali Baba laughed. He had really fooled his parents.

"Do you remember the story of the boy who called wolf?" asked Mr. Bernstein. "If you try and trick us now, no one will believe you if you ever do see a real bear."

So Ali Baba kept watch for a bear. And he began to keep score of the animals he did see:

moose	17	marmot	1
buffalo	39	antelope	8
beavers	3	deer	12
gophers	61	coyote	1

He didn't bother to count mosquitoes. They had mosquitoes at home.

There were many things to do in the park. One morning, they got up extra early and took a ride on a rubber raft on the Snake River. Everyone, even Ali Baba who had passed his intermediate swimming test the summer before, had to wear bright orange life vests. It was very quiet out on the water. The splashing of the oars made the only sound. The guide told them to listen carefully. Soon they could hear the sounds of birds calling and animals grazing near the water.

"I see a bear!" Ali Baba called out. The hair stood up on his arms, and his heart began beating rapidly. It was an exciting moment, but it lasted only a second.

What Ali Baba saw wasn't a bear at all. It was a large tree stump. "I really thought it was a bear," Ali Baba protested. He hadn't been trying to fool anyone this time. He felt silly making a mistake like that. The other people on the raft all laughed.

"It's pretty hard to find a bear around here these days," said the guide. "That stump is just the color of a bear. No wonder you got confused." Ali Baba knew he was saying that to make him feel better, but he didn't. He hadn't seen a bear, and he had been careless enough to mistake a tree stump for an animal. A good detective wouldn't do that.

"Is that a bear?" asked Mr. Bernstein a little later. Everyone on the raft turned to look. But it was the back end of a moose half hidden by a bush. Ali Baba smiled at his father. It was nice to see that other people made mistakes.

That afternoon, the family went horseback riding. Mr. Bernstein was the only one in the family who had ever ridden a horse before. Mrs. Bernstein was very nervous. Ali Baba felt a little scared himself, but he would never admit it. He wondered what would happen if a bear approached. Would it frighten his horse? Would he fall off?

19

"Are there any bears around here?" he asked the man in charge of the horses.

"If there were, the horses would smell them long before we could spot them," said the man. "The bears like to be left alone. They don't come where there are so many people and other animals."

So Ali Baba spent the next hour concentrating on riding and not on bears. It was a lot of fun, and he couldn't wait to go home and brag to Roger about his newest accomplishment. Still, even though he was having such a good time, Ali Baba wished he would see a bear before he went home. Perhaps he would have better luck at Yellowstone National Park, he thought as they drove to the second park.

Just as before, whenever they were driving along and they saw a group of parked cars, Mr. Bernstein would pull off along the side of the road, too. Parked cars usually meant that someone had spotted animals in the area. Ali Baba kept watching for a bear.

"Is there a bear?" Ali Baba always wanted to know.

"I saw a bear yesterday," said a boy who appeared to be a year or two older than Ali Baba.

"So did I," said Ali Baba. He was about to add that the bear he had seen turned out to be only a stump of an old tree. However, the older boy interrupted him.

"Hey, that's neat," the boy said, smiling at Ali Baba. "It's getting really hard to see a bear around here these days. There're just a few of us who have done it. You must have good eyes, like me."

Ali Baba felt trapped. There was no way he could change his statement now.

"Aaaah, yeah," he mumbled.

"Where do you come from?" the boy asked.

"St. Paul, Minnesota," said Ali Baba. The words just flew out of his mouth even though they weren't true.

"I'm from Worthington, Ohio," the boy said. "My name's Greg. What's yours?"

Having already told two lies, even if one was not intentional, there was no way Ali Baba was going to identify himself. He couldn't even say his name was David, which was vague enough, as there were so many Davids in the United States.

"Larry," he said. The name just popped into his head. Ali Baba didn't know anyone named Larry, and he didn't know why he picked that name.

Luckily, at that moment, Greg's parents called him to get back into their car. They were ready to drive on.

"See you around," said Greg.

"Yeah," said Ali Baba, hoping that they would never meet again.

That evening at supper, there was a family with two small boys sitting at the next table in the park cafeteria.

"You know what?" one of them said to Ali Baba.

"What?"

"There's a kid around here named Barry, and he saw a bear."

"Really?" asked Ali Baba. He didn't feel he had to impress these two boys. And besides, he still felt uncomfortable about the story he made up to tell Greg.

"Yeah. He comes from St. Charles. That's in Missouri near where we live."

That made two guys who had seen bears, Greg and Barry. Ali Baba wished he had been that lucky.

The next day, Ali Baba sat eating an ice-cream cone when he was approached by a little girl of about five or six.

"Did you see any bears?" asked the girl.

"No," said Ali Baba. "Did you?"

"No. But there must be one around, 'cause some boy named Harry saw two of them."

"Really? How do you know?" asked Ali Baba.

"Some kids told me. Harry came here from St. Matthews. That's in Kentucky where I live."

Ali Baba licked his ice-cream cone thoughtfully. Either there were a lot more bears around than he had thought, or else there were no bears at all. It was a curious coincidence that Harry and Barry both came from cities that started with the word *Saint.* In fact, when he thought of it, so did Larry, the fellow he had invented. Larry came from St. Paul. Ali Baba was sure he was onto something now.

Ali Baba walked over to his father. Mr. Bernstein was comparing cameras with another man. A young girl stood beside the man, and she looked at Ali Baba. "Have you seen any bears?" he asked her.

The girl shook her head. "No," she said. "But I heard about another girl named Mary, just like me, and she saw a bear."

"I bet she lives in St. Paul or St. Matthews or somewhere like that," guessed Ali Baba.

"I don't know where she lives," said the Mary who stood along side of him.

Ali Baba started counting on his fingers: Larry, Barry, Harry, Mary. . . . He wondered how many other names there were that rhymed: Jerry, Carrie, Gary, Terry. He bet there were dozens of cities that sounded alike, too.

So when Ali Baba was ten years, two months, and seventeen days old, he returned home from a trip to Wyoming without having seen a single bear. However, he had solved a mystery that no one but he even knew existed. He had seen how a single accidental lapse from the truth had grown into a group of kids and a bunch of bears.

It was something to bear in mind for the future.

3. ALI BABA
MAKES A FIND

One summer afternoon, when Ali Baba Bernstein was ten years, two months, and twenty-four days old, he was walking along the street with his friend Roger. The boys were headed to a new video store where they were going to study the films. That way, the next time they had money to rent one, they would know what they wanted to get.

Suddenly, in the midst of their discussion about whether it was better to rent a film they had already seen and liked or a new one that neither of them knew, Ali Baba spotted something out of the corner of his eye. It was a small piece of paper lying on the sidewalk. In size and color, it resembled a wadded-up dollar bill. Automatically, without changing his stride, Ali Baba reached down and picked up the bit of paper.

He was always collecting bits and pieces of things from the street. When he walked with his mother, she scolded him for handling all that garbage. But Roger was used to Ali Baba and his habit of stopping to examine everything. He understood that if Ali Baba was going to become a detective, he had to keep his eyes open and check out any suspicious or curious objects that he found. One man's garbage might be another man's clue. On their last walk down this very street a few days ago, Ali Baba had found a broken key, an empty envelope, a plumbing nut, half a pipe, and a nickel.

"What did you find now?" asked Roger.

Ali Baba shrugged his shoulders. He held the paper in his fist without opening it.

"Oh, nothing. Just a bit of paper," he said. But even without studying the piece of paper,

Ali Baba was pretty sure he knew what he had picked up. He thought it was a dollar bill that had been folded several times. If he told Roger about it, he'd probably want to share it. Ali Baba had already spent his whole allowance for the week. He could sure use an extra dollar. So Ali Baba stuck his hand in his pants pocket and dropped the folded piece of paper inside.

"Just a second," said Roger as the boys approached Cheese Heaven, the shop that Roger's father owned. "I want to leave my sweatshirt here. My mother made me take it, but it's too hot to wear."

"I'll wait outside," said Ali Baba. Roger knew that he didn't care for the smell of imported cheeses. He had another reason for waiting outside, too. He wanted to take a peek at the lump of paper. And he didn't want Roger to see him doing it.

Finding a dollar bill was certainly great luck. Ali Baba had never found more than a quarter at one time. For a moment, he rubbed his fingers over the paper inside his pocket and savored the possibility of his good fortune before he actually looked to see what he was hiding.

He pulled it out and slowly unfolded the paper. It certainly looked like real money. He turned it over carefully. He blinked and looked again. The picture in the middle of the bill was vaguely familiar, but it wasn't George Washington. It certainly wasn't Abraham Lincoln. The man didn't have a beard. Ali Baba looked closely to read the small print below the picture. It said *Franklin.* Of course, it was a picture of Benjamin Franklin. He should have recognized him. They had studied all about him at school. Then Ali Baba froze with shock. In each of the four corners of the bill was not the number one he expected, but the number 100. He had found a hundred-dollar bill. He was rich! It was about the most thrilling moment of his life. Imagine finding a hundred-dollar bill on the sidewalk. Had any ten-year-old boy in the history of the world ever found a hundred-dollar bill? Wait till his mother heard about this. She would never scold him for picking up garbage again.

Ali Baba turned and looked around to see if anyone was watching him. His mind was suddenly filled with questions. Had anyone seen him pick up the bill? Well, Roger had, but he didn't count. Why was a hundred-

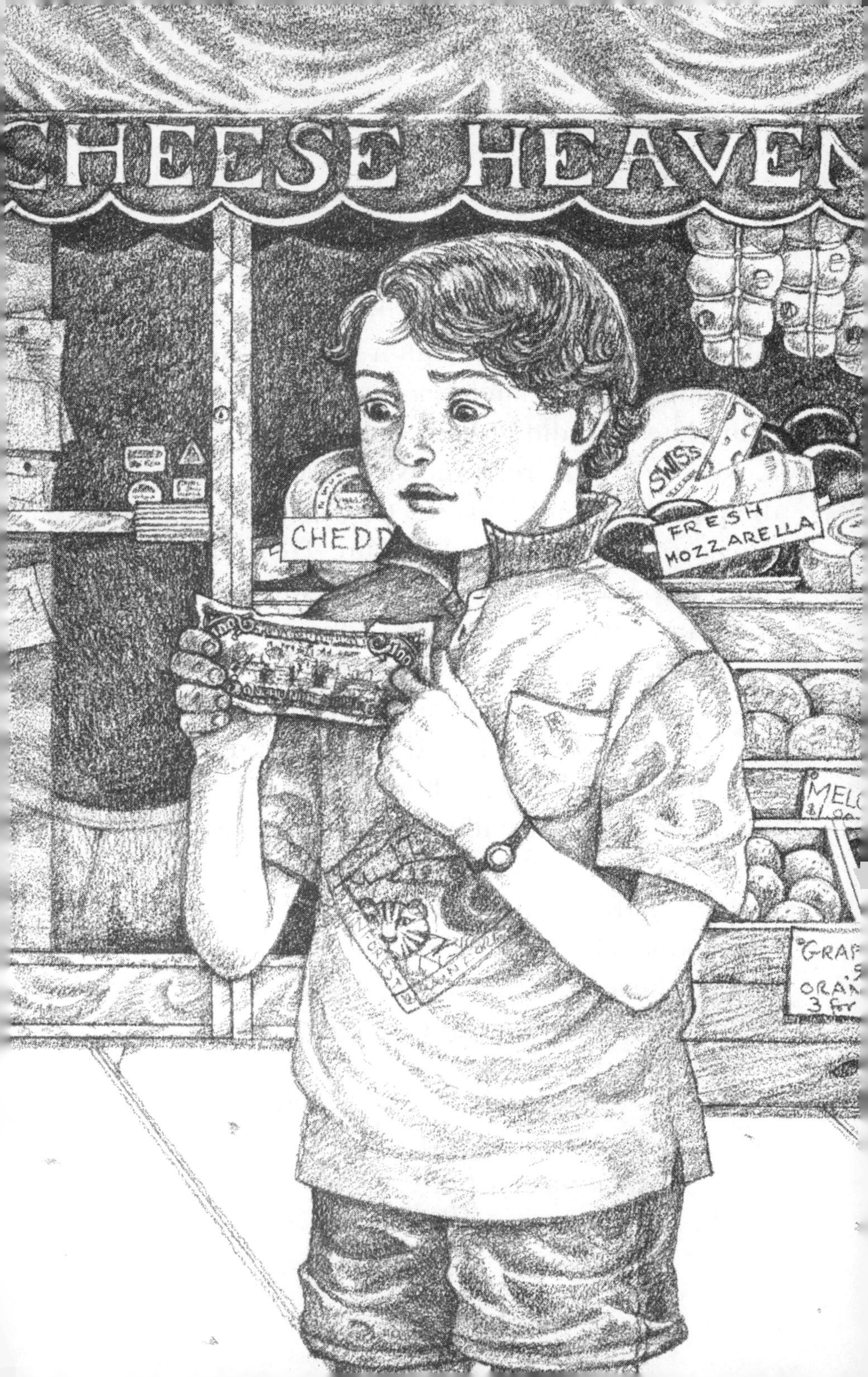
CHEESE HEAVEN
CHEDD
SWISS
FRESH MOZZARELLA

dollar bill lying on the sidewalk? Was it real or was it counterfeit? Who had it belonged to? Would he have to give it back? Was it his now?

"Here," said Roger, coming out of the store and waving a chocolate bar in his hand. "This is from my father." In addition to a large variety of cheeses, Cheese Heaven also sold imported chocolates.

Ali Baba squeezed his fist with the hundred-dollar bill shut and hurriedly put it back inside his pocket.

"What was that?" asked Roger.

"What was what?" mumbled Ali Baba, bus-ily opening the paper on the chocolate bar that Roger had handed him.

"What you put in your pocket. What was it?" asked Roger.

"Nothing," said Ali Baba. He crammed half of the candy bar into his mouth and returned the rest to Roger. Ali Baba could hardly taste the candy. Here he was, eating his friend's chocolate and hiding something from him at the same time. Why should he have to share with Roger? He was the one who found the hundred-dollar bill. Didn't that make it his alone? But Roger was his best friend. He could think later about sharing the money. Now he would share the news.

Ali Baba swallowed the chocolate. "Look at this," he said to Roger. His voice was thick with emotion and chocolate. He took the bill out of his pocket. As they walked along, Roger looked at the paper.

"Wow," he gasped. "Do you think it's real?"

"I don't know," whispered Ali Baba. "I never saw a hundred-dollar bill before. If it's real, I'm rich."

"Are you going to keep it?" asked Roger, echoing the very thoughts that were running through his friend's head.

"I don't know," said Ali Baba. "Maybe this money was lost by someone."

"Of course it was lost by someone, dummy," said Roger. "Why else would it be lying in the street?"

"I mean, maybe it was lost by someone who really needs it. Someone who is starving. Maybe one of those homeless men we sometimes see."

"Those people don't have hundred-dollar bills," said Roger.

That was true. Only very rich people walked

around with hundred-dollar bills in their pockets.

"We could rent a whole lot of films with all this money," said Roger. "We could get all your favorites and all mine, too. And we could rent loads of new ones that neither of us has ever seen."

"I have to think about how to spend it," said Ali Baba.

"We don't have to spend it all in one place. We could go for ice-cream sundaes first. With a hundred dollars, we could stop at just about every store along the street and still have money left over," said Roger eagerly.

"Maybe," said Ali Baba. He folded up the bill and held it tightly in his fist. Then he opened it up and studied it again. He could hardly believe it was real.

A thought occurred to him. "If I went into a store with a hundred-dollar bill, they'd be very suspicious."

"Why?" asked Roger. "Do you think it's fake?"

"I can't tell," said Ali Baba. "Even if it's real, no one expects boys our age to have so much money."

"Tell them your father gave it to you," suggested Roger.

"But he didn't," Ali Baba pointed out. Just because he had been lucky enough to find so much money, he didn't think he should have to start lying about it. "Anyway, they wouldn't believe me. They'd probably think I stole it."

"I'll tell them you didn't," said Roger.

"That won't be good enough. Why should anyone believe you? They'll think you are my accomplice."

Roger nodded his head. "You're right," he agreed. "I hadn't thought about that. I guess you have to give it back."

"Give it back? To who?" asked Ali Baba. "I don't know who it belongs to. It could have been lying in the street for days." He thought a minute. "I wish it was a ten-dollar bill instead of a hundred."

"Why?" asked Roger. "That's the stupidest thing I ever heard."

"No, it isn't," said Ali Baba. "If it was ten dollars, we wouldn't have to worry about whether it was real or fake. And if it was ten dollars, I wouldn't have to worry about who it belongs to. And if it was ten dollars, we could stop at any store we were passing and we could spend the money, and that would be that. But a hundred-dollar bill . . ." Ali Baba lowered his voice and turned around to see if anyone was listening to their conversation. "A hundred-dollar bill is a big responsibility. I don't know what to do. I've got to think about this some more."

"Yeah, I see what you mean," said Roger.

The boys had come to the video store.

"I'm not interested in looking at videos anymore," said Ali Baba.

"That's okay," said Roger. "What do you want to do instead?"

Ali Baba thought for a minute. He realized that a hundred-dollar bill wasn't something he could walk around with forever. And if he wasn't careful, perhaps he would lose it, too. Imagining the way he would feel if he lost the hundred-dollar bill made Ali Baba realize that at this very moment someone might be feeling just that way because they had.

"Let's go to the police station. Maybe someone went to them and reported it missing," he said.

"Do we have to?" asked Roger.

"Yes," said Ali Baba sadly. "It's the only thing to do."

At least it was interesting to be going to the police station. Ali Baba and Roger had never been there. However, it turned out to look more like an office than anything else—just like on television, too. A tall policeman with a dark mustache named James Connor listened to Ali Baba's story and examined the bill.

"It's real, all right," he said. "And you're good kids to bring this here. You did the responsible thing."

As the officer put the bill inside a tan envelope, Ali Baba wished being responsible wasn't so disappointing. He had been secretly hoping that he would be told he could keep the money.

"You're a lucky kid," said the police officer, smiling at Ali Baba.

"You mean I can keep it, after all?" asked Ali Baba with delight.

"Well, we'll have to hold on to it for a couple of weeks in case someone contacts us about it. But I think that's pretty unlikely. Give me your phone number, and we'll call you when it's time for you to come and pick it up."

"Fantastic," said Roger, whistling loudly. It

was a new trick of his and one that Ali Baba
wished he could master, too.

Before the day came to claim the money, Ali
Baba made an important decision. He decided to split the money with Roger.

Roger thought this was a great idea.

"If you had found it when we were walking
together, you'd split it with me, wouldn't
you?" asked Ali Baba.

"I sure would. In fact, I'm going to start
looking for a hundred-dollar bill right now,"
said Roger.

A few months ago, Ali Baba's arithmetic
class had been talking about probability. He
knew the odds were very, very slight that his
friend would find a hundred-dollar bill in the
near future. Still, fifty dollars was a lot of
money for a boy ten years, three months, and
seven days old.

Ali Baba, Roger, and Ali Baba's mother
went to the police station, where James Connor smiled and handed Ali Baba the envelope
containing the hundred-dollar bill. Then they
went to the bank and exchanged the bill for
smaller bills.

Walking home, they passed the church on
the corner of Broadway and 114th Street

where free meals were provided for people who were hungry. Ali Baba realized that he was an awfully lucky kid. "Just a minute," he said, and ran inside, leaving his mother and Roger on the sidewalk. Ali Baba looked around the soup kitchen for the person in charge and handed her half of his share of the hundred dollars.

"What an angel you are!" she exclaimed, giving Ali Baba a big hug. "Twenty-five dollars will help feed many hungry people."

Ali Baba blushed and left quickly.

"What was that about?" asked Roger when Ali Baba came out of the church.

"Oh, nothing," said Ali Baba. "Let's get going."

But as they walked home, he was happy. Sometimes, being responsible wasn't disappointing at all. In fact, he felt just great.

4. ALI BABA AND THE MISSING GLASS SLIPPER

The occupants of apartment 8A in the building where Ali Baba lived were Doris and Simon Glass and their two-year-old daughter, Amanda. Mr. and Mrs. Glass were friends of Ali Baba's parents. Ali Baba was polite to his parents' friends, but they didn't particularly interest him. And of course, Amanda was much too young.

But they also had a dog. It was only a small and stupid dachshund, however it still intrigued him. Naturally, Ali Baba preferred clever dogs like bloodhounds and German shepherds that were good at sniffing for mysterious scents. He also admired Saint Bernard dogs that could rescue you if you were lost in a snowstorm. Little dogs like miniature dachshunds weren't good for much. Still, walking even a small dog would be a good cover for a boy who was following a suspicious person.

From time to time, Ali Baba reminded his parents that he wanted a dog. They both kept maintaining that it was too big a responsibility for him. Here was little Amanda, though, and she had a dog. Of course, the dog belonged to her parents, but when she got just a bit older, she would help take care of the dog, too. If she could do it, he certainly could. All he needed was a way to prove it.

When Ali Baba was ten years, three months, and eight days old, he and his parents happened to meet the Glass family out in the street. The Glasses were getting ready to go off on a trip, and they were discussing their plans.

"We put Slipper in a kennel last time, and she was just miserable," said Mrs. Glass.

Slipper was the name of the Glass dog.

40

"She lost weight and looked terrible by the time we came home," said Mr. Glass.

"That's too bad," said Mrs. Bernstein, clicking her tongue and trying to appear sympathetic.

"How come your dog has such a funny name?" Ali Baba wanted to know. If he had a dog, he would give it a more macho name.

"When we first got her, she was just the size of Simon's bedroom slippers and the same color, too. She lay down on the floor next to his slippers, and you could hardly tell which was the dog and which was a leather slipper," said Doris Glass, smiling fondly at the memory.

"Except that my slippers didn't have a tail to wag," said Simon Glass. "Anyhow, what we were wondering," he continued, "is if you would take care of our dog while we're away. We'll be gone only a week, and we thought Ali Baba might like the chance to walk and play with a dog."

"Sure," said Ali Baba immediately. "I'd love to." He turned to his parents to see how they felt about this possibility. Even though a dachshund wasn't the sort of dog he wanted to get, if he could take care of Slipper for a few days, he'd be able to show his parents that he was responsible enough to have a dog of his own.

"Our apartment is rather small for a dog," said Mrs. Bernstein hesitantly.

"Slipper is a very small dog," Ali Baba pointed out.

"That's right," said Mr. Glass, smiling at Ali Baba.

"Dogs often make a mess," said Mr. Bernstein, knowing that his wife wasn't keen on a dog, even if it was only for one week.

"Does Slipper make a mess?" Ali Baba asked their neighbors.

"Oh, no," Mr. and Mrs. Glass both said at once. "Actually," Mrs. Glass said, "I suppose you could even let her stay in our apartment. Except that she'd get so lonely all day by herself. She's a very friendly dog, and that's why she was unhappy at the kennel. No one talked to her all the days that we were away."

"How do you talk to a dog?" asked Mrs. Bernstein. "Do you bark?"

Mr. and Mrs. Glass laughed. They thought Mrs. Bernstein was making a joke, but Ali

Baba knew she was serious. In fact, it was something that he wondered about himself.

"You just talk to her the way you would to Ali Baba. Of course, she can't answer you. But she is a highly intelligent dog and likes to be spoken to," explained Mrs. Glass.

"And if you all go out and leave her in the house, then you can turn on the television. She especially likes the game show contestants who jump up and down and squeal when they win a lot of prizes," said Mr. Glass.

Ali Baba was just about to suggest that the Glasses could leave their television on when they went away. Then he realized that arrangement would work against him. He really wanted Slipper to stay in his apartment.

So in the end, it was all settled. The Glass family was going off on their vacation, and Slipper, the Glass dachshund, was going to spend the time visiting with the Bernsteins.

On the morning they were departing, Mr. Glass brought Slipper downstairs. He detached the leash and showed Ali Baba how it worked. He gave Ali Baba a large bag of dog food and explained that Slipper was fed only once a day and only from the contents of the bag. "No scraps. No table food," he said. "But please be sure to have fresh water out at all times." Mr. Glass had even brought Slipper's two bowls along. "She eats from the red one. Her water goes in the blue one," he concluded.

Ali Baba wondered what would happen if he put the water in the red bowl instead of the blue one. Even though he was tempted, he decided that he would not experiment. He wanted everything to go just fine. He wanted Slipper to have a happy time visiting, and he wanted his parents to enjoy the presence of the dog in their apartment. Then, maybe by his next birthday, they would agree to get a dog of their own.

After Mr. Glass left, Slipper settled herself down in a corner by the door. What a dumb dog, Ali Baba thought to himself. She doesn't even realize she is in a strange apartment. A bloodhound would have gone sniffing for clues right away.

Shortly after Slipper's arrival, Mrs. Bernstein suggested to her son that he take the dog for a walk. So that is how it came to be that on the morning that Ali Baba Bernstein was ten years, three months, and twelve days old, he was heading for the street holding on to a leash with Slipper Glass at the other end.

He felt a little silly walking such a small, undistinguished dog as Slipper. He would have much preferred holding the leash of a bloodhound or a Saint Bernard. Still, as Ali Baba had never walked any dog before this very moment, it did make him feel a little bit special. He decided that he would walk up toward Broadway. But as soon as they were outside, Slipper gave a strong tug on her leash and set off toward Amsterdam Avenue. He was surprised that Slipper cared about which direction their walk took them.

Ali Baba went where Slipper led. He waved to a couple of people that he recognized, but he couldn't stop to speak to anyone. Slipper obviously knew her mind. Probably this was her usual route when she went for a walk with either Mr. or Mrs. Glass, he decided.

"Hey, Ali Baba," a voice called out.

Ali Baba turned around. It was Natalie Gomez, a girl who lived on his street.

"I didn't know you had a dog," Natalie said, running to keep up with Ali Baba and Slipper.

"I don't," said Ali Baba. He explained to Natalie how he happened to be holding a

dog's leash. "But maybe someday I'll get a dog, too," he told her.

"I have a cat," said Natalie. "You don't have to walk cats."

She followed along, talking to Ali Baba as they continued. He was so busy watching Slipper that he forgot to feel self-conscious. Natalie had a crush on him, which was flattering, but also embarrassing.

When he was back upstairs again, Ali Baba checked the water bowl for Slipper. It was too early to feed her. She ate her single meal of the day at supper time.

The phone rang, and it was Roger Zucker calling to speak to Ali Baba. The boys made a date to get together the next day. After Ali Baba got off the phone, he took his library book and read for a while. The book was called *The Incredible Journey*, and it was an exciting story of two dogs and a cat that traveled hundreds of miles to find their owner. As he read, Ali Baba heard the doorbell ring a couple of times, but he was so absorbed in his book that he didn't go to see who was at the door. Whoever was there had probably come to see his mother, anyhow. That's the way it usually was.

When Ali Baba finished his book, he went looking for Slipper. He began by looking near the door where she had stationed herself earlier. Slipper seemed to have abandoned her former resting spot in favor of a new one. But where was the new one? He looked behind the sofa in the living room, and in all four corners of the room.

"Mom, have you seen Slipper?" he asked, walking into the kitchen.

"No," said Mrs. Bernstein. "She was here when Mrs. Salmon came by to borrow some cinnamon. I remember because Mrs. Salmon commented on how surprised she was that we had a dog." Mrs. Bernstein thought for a moment. "I don't remember if she was here when the United Parcel delivery man brought me a package."

"Slipper must be hiding," said Ali Baba, grinning at the challenge. He set off to search for the dog.

It was fun at first. Ali Baba looked under his bed and under his parents' bed, as well. He looked in the bathroom. He looked in all the closets and behind all the furniture. He looked in every corner, and still he couldn't find Slipper.

When he played hide and seek with his friends, they could always call, "Come out, come out wherever you are." But Slipper wouldn't respond to that.

Although it wasn't time for Slipper's lone meal of the day, Ali Baba decided to fill her bowl with food. He hoped she would hear the sound and come out of her hiding place. Even after the bowl was filled and waiting, however, Slipper remained hidden.

Ali Baba began to worry. What if Slipper refused to come out of hiding all week long? Or worse. What if somehow she had really gotten lost?

"Slipper is missing," he told his mother.

"How could she be missing? That's impossible," Mrs. Bernstein said.

"Then you find her. I give up," said Ali Baba crossly. What was the fun of having a dog if she had hidden herself away?

"She's probably sleeping somewhere in the apartment," said Mrs. Bernstein. "You'll see. She'll come out and surprise us before you know it."

Ali Baba knew his mother was relieved that the dog wasn't making a mess in the apartment.

By midafternoon, Mrs. Bernstein was no longer so sure that the dog was asleep in the apartment. It was time for Slipper to go for another walk. "I don't want any accidents in the house," she said.

"Maybe she ran out of the house when you opened the door for the man with the parcel or for Mrs. Salmon," said Ali Baba.

"I suppose it's possible," said Mrs. Bernstein. "I'm not used to having a dog around, so I didn't shut the door quickly."

"If she got out, she may be out on the street."

Mrs. Bernstein looked worried. "I don't know how we'll explain to Doris and Simon Glass that we lost their dog the very first day she was with us. They'll never forgive us."

"I'll go outside and look," said Ali Baba. Now that his mother agreed that Slipper wasn't in the apartment, this was becoming a real mystery.

He grabbed the leash so that if he found Slipper, he could attach it to her collar. Ali Baba went out to the hallway and pressed the button for the elevator. Then it occurred to him that if he was to look for the dog, he should think and act like a dog. And no dog, especially no dog as small as Slipper, could reach the elevator button. If Slipper had gone outside, she would have had to walk down the stairs.

Ali Baba felt more and more excited by this mystery of the missing dog. He was convinced that he would find Slipper in the stairwell between two floors. He walked down the steps that connected the sixth floor with the fifth. Then he stopped at the fifth-floor landing and looked around for a sign of Slipper. There was no trace of her. He repeated his search down the steps and at each floor down to the ground floor.

In the lobby, he saw Charlie, the building janitor, and ran to him. "Did you see a dog? I'm looking for Slipper. She's the dachshund that belongs to the Glass family. She's staying in our apartment, but somehow she got lost," he explained.

"I didn't see her," said Charlie. "But I'll keep a lookout. Do you think she's out on the street?"

Ali Baba didn't know, but he ran out hoping to find the dog. He ran toward Amsterdam Avenue, which was where Slipper had pulled him earlier in the day. Though he looked up and down the street, there was no Slipper in sight. Suppose some people had found her and taken her to their home?

Ali Baba remembered that from time to time he would see notices attached to the streetlights. Usually, they were about lost dogs or cats. Whenever he saw one of those signs, he wondered who had posted it. Now he thought he would be the person who was going to put a sign up.

Ali Baba ran back to his house. He would have to get out some paper and markers to make some signs. He took the elevator back to the sixth floor and was just about to go to his apartment when he realized something. In *The Incredible Journey,* the animals walked hundreds of miles to get home. Maybe Slipper was trying to get home, too. Before, when he had gone looking for Slipper, he had assumed that the dog had gone downstairs. Suppose she had walked up instead. But the floors of the apartment building all looked the same. Slipper could easily get lost.

Immediately, Ali Baba ran to the stairwell and began to climb to the seventh floor. It would not be easy for Slipper to climb up or down with her tiny legs. On the landing of the seventh floor, Ali Baba looked around, but he saw nothing except a newspaper waiting to be picked up in front of apartment 7C. He continued his climb up to the next floor. Something dark was lying by the door of 8A, the Glass's apartment. Ali Baba raced down the hallway.

There, in front of apartment 8A, was the curled-up and sleeping body of Slipper.

"What are you doing here?" Ali Baba asked the dog as he snapped the leash onto her collar.

Of course, Slipper didn't give an answer. Ali Baba didn't expect one. Besides, he knew the answer. Slipper had found her way home. Ali Baba felt good about Slipper. And he felt good about himself, too. He had solved a mystery, just like a real detective. Ali Baba stopped on the sixth floor to tell his mother the good news.

"Thank goodness!" said Mrs. Bernstein. She was very relieved.

Then Ali Baba took the dog for her afternoon walk. As he passed the streetlights on the block, he was glad that he wouldn't have to post a message on one of them, after all.

"Dogs have good instincts and good

noses," said Mr. Bernstein that evening. "Slipper must have slipped out of our apartment when the door was opened for a minute, and then she smelled her way back upstairs."

Ali Baba sniffed hard. He could smell a faint whiff of the meat loaf his mother had cooked for the family's supper. He wondered if he could find his way home by sniffing and smelling if he was ever far away and lost. He doubted it.

"She's really very smart," he said to his father. "Maybe she could help me solve some mysteries." Ali Baba had only six days left before the Glass family returned home and claimed their dog. Still, who knew what mysterious events might happen tomorrow. Every day was a potential adventure for a boy like Ali Baba Bernstein.

5. ALI BABA BERNSTEIN, LOST AND FOUND

One morning when Ali Baba Bernstein was ten years, four months, and eleven days old, he went shopping with his mother. It was Ali Baba's least favorite activity in the whole world. In fact, Ali Baba thought that taking an arithmetic test at school was better than shopping. After all, an arithmetic test lasted only about half an hour. Even going to the dentist was an improvement on shopping. A dentist appointment rarely took more than twenty minutes, and it was certainly less painful than standing around while his mother was making a purchase. Mrs. Bernstein liked to compare products and prices. So no matter what she was buying, she always took a long time.

Today was just a half-day of school because the teachers were having a conference. As soon as Ali Baba finished his lunch, Mrs. Bernstein was taking him shopping for a microwave oven. Could anything be worse?

Ali Baba and his mother took the subway to midtown Manhattan where the department stores and the electronics stores were located. "Stay close to me," Mrs. Bernstein instructed her son. She grabbed his hand as the subway train pulled into the station. "I don't want you to get lost."

"I won't get lost," said Ali Baba crossly. He felt like a baby holding his mother's hand, and he was glad when they sat down on the train and his mother let go.

"Which store are we going to first?" asked Ali Baba.

"Macy's," his mother said. "They are having a sale, and I want to see their units and compare them with those at a couple of other stores in the area."

Ali Baba sighed.

The subway train rattled along through the dark tunnel, and Ali Baba looked about him. He read some of the advertisements over-head, and he studied the people on the train. He tried to guess, as he always did when he rode the subway, where they were going. The train stopped, and some passengers got off and others got on. Then the doors closed, and the train started off once more. Ali Baba no-ticed that his mother had closed her eyes. He wondered if she was thinking about mi-crowaves or if she had dozed off. The subway train made so much noise that it would seem impossible for anyone to fall asleep. But sev-eral of the other passengers seemed to have their eyes closed. Maybe the movement of the train rocked them to sleep.

The train pulled into the next station, and again some people got off while others got on. Suddenly, Mrs. Bernstein opened her eyes. "This is Thirty-fourth Street. It's our stop," she shouted to Ali Baba as she jumped up. She pushed her way past a couple of people and out the door. But for once, she forgot to grab her son by the hand, and although Ali Baba had jumped up after her, the door shut

before he reached it. Mrs. Bernstein was outside the subway train, and Ali Baba was inside.

Mrs. Bernstein banged on the door, and one of the passengers tried to pull the door open. When the train began to move, Ali Baba realized he was about to have a big adventure.

"Get off at the next stop," Mrs. Bernstein shouted as the train pulled out of the station. "I'll meet you."

"What did she say?" Ali Baba asked a woman who was standing next to the door.

"She wants you to get out at the next stop," the woman explained. "It's very simple. This train is going downtown. At the next stop, you get off the train and walk up the stairs. Then you go down another flight of stairs and take the uptown train back to Thirty-fourth Street. It won't cost you any more money, either."

"Last week I was reading my newspaper, and I missed my stop. I had to turn around and ride back just like that," said an elderly man.

"I always miss my stop when I'm reading," said someone else.

Ali Baba nodded his head. The train was pulling into the Twenty-third Street station. His adventure was about to start.

"So long," several of the passengers called out to Ali Baba.

"Don't worry. You'll find her," said the woman who had told Ali Baba about going up and down the stairs.

Ali Baba didn't think he was worried. The funny feeling he felt in his stomach was more excitement than fear. Still, it was amazing to think that after all the trips he had taken on the subway with his parents, now he was finally on his own.

Ali Baba joined the other people who were walking up the stairs from the subway. At the top of the flight of stairs, he looked for another stairway that would lead him to the uptown train. He saw it almost at once and immediately walked down the steps. Unfortunately, a train heading uptown was just pulling out of the station. He would probably have to wait about five or ten minutes until another train came. From Twenty-third to Thirty-fourth Street was not so very far. He could probably walk the distance by the time the next train came. For a moment, Ali Baba considered this possibility. Then he realized that his mother was waiting for him at the other subway platform, so it made sense to wait for the train even if it took a few minutes longer.

Ali Baba felt proud. He wondered if any of the passengers waiting on the platform with him thought it strange to see such a young person traveling alone in the middle of the day. A transit police officer walked by, but he didn't question Ali Baba. He didn't even seem to look at him at all. That made Ali Baba feel extra good. I must look so grown-up, Ali Baba said to himself, he thinks I'm about twelve or thirteen years old. He probably thinks I always ride the subway by myself. Still, he wished he was already back at Thirty-fourth Street with his mother. It was odd, but he thought he would really rather be looking at microwave ovens than standing by himself on this subway platform.

At last, another uptown train pulled into the station. Ali Baba got onto the train. As his train pulled out, he saw another train on the opposite track pulling in. For a moment, Ali Baba thought he saw his mother getting off that train. But that was probably just his imagination. She had said she would meet him on the platform at Thirty-fourth Street.

Ali Baba couldn't find his mother on the

Thirty-fourth Street platform. He walked back and forth, from one end of the platform to the other, several times. How could his mother have gotten lost in such a short time? he wondered.

Then it occurred to Ali Baba that his mother must have gone to Macy's and was waiting for him there. That made sense. Why would she want to waste time just standing around in the dimly lit and noisy subway station? If she waited for him at Macy's, she could look at the microwave ovens at the same time.

Ali Baba walked up the two flights of stairs that led to the street. When he reached the street level, it was easy to locate Macy's. It was a huge department store, and there was an enormous sign attached to the building. Even a four-year-old could find Macy's, he thought. Of course his mother expected him to find her there.

Ali Baba crossed the street and went through the revolving door into the store. He had to ask about six different people before he was told on which floor he would find the microwaves. Electronic equipment was on the fifth floor, he learned.

Ali Baba took the escalators up and up. But reaching the correct floor was not enough. Then he had to ask about six more people where the microwaves were located. It was amazing how big the store was and how many things there were to buy. It was also amazing how many people had come to shop. Unfortunately for Ali Baba, microwave ovens were not on the fifth floor. They were in the basement where kitchenware was sold.

Ali Baba rode the escalators down. Finally, he found the right place. There were about a dozen different microwave ovens on display. Ali Baba didn't bother to examine them. Instead, he walked around and around the area searching for his mother. He saw one woman who even looked just like her—from the back. He ran up to her and was just about to grab her arm when he realized that she was wearing a dress he had never seen before. They hadn't been separated long enough for his mother to buy a new dress. And on closer inspection, Ali Baba saw that the woman really didn't look like his mother at all.

He turned away quickly, so the woman wouldn't realize that he had mistaken her for someone else. Where could his mother be?

She wasn't on the subway platform, and she wasn't in the store. Could she have gone back home? Maybe that's where she thought she would meet him. Back home.

Ali Baba put his hands in his pockets. He had a broken pencil, a nickel, and two pennies in one pocket, and a crumpled tissue in the other. He didn't have enough money to take the subway back home. There was just one thing to do. He would have to walk.

He wondered if his mother had made it home already. In that case, what he ought to do was phone her and tell her he was on his way home, too. Then she wouldn't have to worry about him. His mother was awfully good at worrying. Even though he didn't have enough money for a telephone call, he found a phone booth out on the street. His father had once told him that if he punched the "0" button before dialing a number, he could call home collect. That meant the person he was calling would pay for the telephone call. So that was exactly what Ali Baba did now. Only when the phone rang at his home, no one answered. His mother hadn't gotten home yet, after all.

As Ali Baba was about to begin his walk

home, he had another idea. He would phone his father. Often when his mother was worried about something, she called his father. If she got home and was worried about Ali Baba, she might call Mr. Bernstein. And if Ali Baba left a message with his father, he could relay it to her. Once again, Ali Baba punched the "0" button, and this time he dialed his father's number.

Mr. Bernstein was not in his office, either. Luckily, however, his business partner was. He accepted the collect call from Ali Baba.

"How are you doing, David?" Mr. Goodman asked.

"I'm fine," said Ali Baba, making a face at the telephone receiver. Hardly anyone called him David anymore. "Could you tell my father to tell my mother that I'm walking home? I'll be there in a little while, so she shouldn't worry."

"Sure," said Mr. Goodman. "Anything else?"

"No," said Ali Baba. "Good-bye." He hung up and left the phone booth.

Luckily, it was a mild and sunny day. And luckily, too, the streets in Manhattan are easy to follow. Even though he had never walked to or from Macy's before, Ali Baba knew it would be impossible to get lost. After Thirty-fourth Street came Thirty-fifth Street. After Thirty-fifth Street came Thirty-sixth. There were hundreds of people walking along the streets, and Ali Baba wondered where they were all going. Were they shopping or going to work? Were they on their way to a restaurant or on their way home? No one seemed the least bit surprised to see a boy of ten years, four months, and eleven days walking along the avenue by himself.

By the time Ali Baba had gone twenty blocks, which was about a mile, he was feeling hungry and thirsty. He was also feeling a bit annoyed with his mother. When he found her, he would refuse to do any shopping today.

There were still fifty-seven blocks to go. Ali Baba walked past a vendor selling frankfurters. The aroma followed him for the next block. He realized that he was not just hungry from all this walking—he was starving. He passed another vendor. This one was selling hot pretzels. If only he had enough money to buy one, he would have the energy to walk a hundred more blocks. But he didn't have the money. Fortunately, he didn't have to walk a hundred more blocks, either.

He trudged along, going slower and slower. If he had someone to talk to, he wouldn't notice how long it took to get to the end of each street. He never noticed streets when he was walking along with Roger or any of his other friends.

Ali Baba wished he could sit down for a few minutes to rest, but there was nowhere to sit. He thought about how good he would feel when he was home at last and sitting down. He thought about how he had sat at his desk in school that morning. He hadn't realized then how lucky he had been to be sitting instead of walking. He wished he was in school now. Even if he was taking an arithmetic test, school would be better than this. He would be in a sitting position, and his feet could take it easy. Ali Baba thought about sitting in other places. Sitting in a movie was the best, but he would even be willing to sit in a dentist's chair. If only he could wish himself into a dentist's chair, that's what he would do.

All this thinking and wishing didn't do his feet much good, but it did pass the time. Ali

Baba saw that he had walked another eight blocks. He kept on going. This was a day to find some money, he thought. If he had found his hundred-dollar bill today, he could have taken a taxi home. He would just stand on the next street corner and wave his arm, as he'd seen his parents do in the past. A taxi would stop in front of him, and he'd open the door and sit down. He'd tell the driver his address, and then he could just take it easy the rest of the way home.

Ali Baba looked at the ground. He actually found a penny. It didn't help his situation at all, but he still picked it up and put it into his pocket.

When he was twenty-five blocks from home, a police car pulled up alongside of Ali Baba. A police officer jumped out and walked over.

"What's your name, son?" the officer asked.

Ali Baba froze. He wondered for a moment if he had broken a law. He couldn't think of anything he had done, but his father had once said to someone, "Ignorance of the law is no excuse." And now, Ali Baba was ignorant of what he had done, and he knew it was no excuse.

"Ali Baba Bernstein. At least that's what I call myself. My birth certificate says David Bernstein," he admitted.

The police officer's frown turned into a grin. "Okay," he said. "Hop into the car."

"What did I do?" asked Ali Baba.

"You got lost," said the officer. "Your mother dialed nine-one-one. She's frantic."

"I'm not lost," said Ali Baba. "I know exactly where I am." He looked up at the street sign. "I'm at Eighty-third Street. I've been walking since Thirty-fourth Street, and I'm on my way home."

"Well, I'll get you home a whole lot faster," said the police officer. "And I'll radio to the station to notify your mother."

Of all the seats that he had imagined sitting in, even a kid with an imagination as good as Ali Baba's could not have thought of a police car.

"Can I sit in front with you?" asked Ali Baba.

"Sorry. Police regulations say you have to sit in the back."

"That's all right," said Ali Baba.

He sat down and looked at the wire grill

that separated him from the officer. "What's this for?" he asked.

"So you can't attack me," said the officer. "If you had a gun, I would have already taken it from you. But you might want to try to choke me or hit me over the head with your shoe or something."

"I wouldn't do that," said Ali Baba.

"Good," said the police officer as the car drove off.

"Can you turn your siren on?" asked Ali Baba. Maybe that was against regulations when it wasn't a matter of life or death.

"Sure. Why not," the officer said. He turned on the siren and began to weave through traffic.

Ali Baba wished that he could somehow be on the outside watching himself on the inside. But since he couldn't, he was pretty satisfied to find himself on the inside. This was certainly his greatest adventure yet.

It took only a very few minutes to reach Ali Baba's home. There was a group of people standing on the sidewalk in front of his apartment building. Ali Baba saw his mother and several of their neighbors. Mr. and Mrs.

Salmon and Mr. Vivaldi were there. And there was his father, too. The police officer opened the door for Ali Baba.

"Oh, here he is!" shouted Mrs. Bernstein as her neighbors let out a loud cheer. "Are you all right?" she asked her son. Mrs. Bernstein ran her hands over his face as if she expected him to look different from the boy she had left on the subway train three hours earlier.

"Of course, I'm all right," said Ali Baba. "Where were you? I looked everywhere, on the subway platform and at Macy's."

"You went to Macy's?" asked his mother, sounding amazed.

"Sure. Why weren't you there?"

"Because you were lost."

"But I never was lost," Ali Baba protested. "You were lost, not me. I always knew exactly where I was. And I even tried to phone you, but you weren't home."

"Well, everyone is found now," said Mr. Bernstein, putting his arm around his son's shoulders. "I knew you could find your way home. But you can't blame your mother for worrying about you."

"For goodness' sake," said Ali Baba. "I'm not a baby. I'm ten years, four months, and eleven days old." He turned to the officer who was standing at the curb beside his car. Ali Baba wanted to ask if he could see his gun close up, but he was sure that would be against regulations. "Could I look at your handcuffs?" he asked instead.

The officer removed the handcuffs that had been attached to his belt and handed them to Ali Baba. "Your mother probably wants to buy a pair of these so she won't lose you again," he said.

Ali Baba made a face at that idea and quickly handed the metal cuffs back to him.

"Well, I guess I can go now." The police officer smiled.

"Wait a minute," said Mr. Salmon. "May I take a picture of you and Ali Baba?"

Ali Baba noticed for the first time that his neighbor had been holding his camera all this time.

"Sure," the officer agreed.

Ali Baba stood up as tall as he could next to the officer. When Mr. Salmon gave him a copy, as he knew he would, he would have proof that all of this happened today. The picture wouldn't show the subway train or Macy's or the long, long walk home. But it

would be a perfect souvenir of his speedy ride along the avenue in the police car. It would be a souvenir of the day his mother was lost and he was found.

6. ALI BABA AND THE BEST GIFT IN THE WORLD

*E*ver since the police told Ali Baba that the hundred-dollar bill he had found was his to keep, he had been thinking about spending his share. There were a lot of things a boy could buy for twenty-five dollars. In fact, Roger had already spent all of his half of the find. He had bought a book of raffle tickets that the school was selling as a fund-raiser. The winner would get a ten-speed bike, and there were runner-up prizes of free movie passes and free ice-cream cones. Roger had also bought two used video-cassettes and three candy bars. He had bought a T-shirt with a picture of his favorite cartoon character, too.

Now Ali Baba was ten years, four months, and twenty days old, and he still hadn't spent any of his money. But he thought about it all the time.

"It's burning a hole in your pocket, isn't it?" asked his father.

That was a funny thing to say. If the money was burning a hole, Ali Baba would be on fire, and there would be smoke all around, too.

"I just mean that you want to get rid of it too fast," explained Mr. Bernstein. "There's no rush for you to spend it. If you use it now, you won't have it next month."

It was amazing to Ali Baba how grown-ups wasted their breath saying things that were ridiculous or obvious.

What Ali Baba really wanted to do with his money was buy a dog. Even though his parents had complimented him recently on the fact that he was becoming more responsible, he wasn't sure how they would react if he walked through the door with a dog on the end of a leash. So the money remained unspent, and Ali Baba remained without a dog.

Then one Tuesday when he was ten years, four months, and twenty-eight days old, Ali Baba's grandmother phoned while his parents were both out of the house. During their conversation, she said, "Next week is your parents' anniversary. They've been married for fifteen years."

"That's a long time," said Ali Baba. He wondered how many months and days made up fifteen years.

"Yes, it is," said his grandmother. "I'm having trouble deciding what to buy them as a gift. In the past, fifteenth anniversary presents were supposed to be made of ivory."

"Ivory?"

"Yes. Traditionally, anniversary gifts are supposed to be made of a different material each year, like paper, china, or glass. The twenty-fifth anniversary is called the silver anniversary. And the fiftieth is gold."

"I didn't know that," said Ali Baba. "But ivory comes from elephants, and they're an endangered species. It's illegal to kill them for their ivory tusks."

"I know," said his grandmother. "Don't worry. I'm not planning to kill an elephant, but I do hope to find something extra special to give to your parents."

When he got off the phone, Ali Baba thought about his parents' anniversary. In the past, he had never given them a present to mark the occasion. Now that he was getting older, he thought he should. The question, of course, was what he could possibly give them. Every year for as long as he could remember, he had gone to the shop owned by Roger's father and had bought his parents imported chocolates for their birthdays. It was an easy way to solve the dilemma of giving presents, and he usually got to eat some of the chocolates, too. But if he wasn't going to spend his money on a dog, he could afford to buy his parents a bigger and more exciting gift for their anniversary.

Although he certainly wasn't going to buy them something made of ivory, maybe he could think of something else.

"Hey, I know what," said Roger when Ali Baba asked him for advice. "Give them Ivory soap."

"Soap?"

"Well, it's *ivory,* isn't it?" asked Roger.

Roger was no help. But then on the way

home from Roger's house, Ali Baba got a good idea. He would find his parents something that was the color of ivory. Something white.

As he was thinking about white gifts, Ali Baba walked past the pet shop on Broadway. There in the window was a white dog. It was perfect! He could use all his money to buy the white dog, name the dog Ivory, and give it to his parents. That way, they would have a special gift for their fifteenth wedding anniversary, and Ali Baba would finally have the dog that he wanted. It would be the best gift in the world.

He walked home full of plans. He could take Ivory for long walks after school. Perhaps while they were walking, he would have some new adventures. He imagined himself and the white dog helping the police solve difficult mysteries. He and the dog would be outside the bank when a robber came running out. The dog would be able to track the robber down by his scent, and Ali Baba would be a witness to the crime.

Ali Baba imagined the newspaper headline as he walked: ALI BABA AND HIS DOG, IVORY, SOLVE ANOTHER MYSTERY FOR THE POLICE.

Actually, Ali Baba didn't care for the name "Ivory." Maybe his parents wouldn't mind if their dog had a different name. He preferred the name "Delancey." It was the name of a street in lower Manhattan, and he thought it would make a good name for a dog, too. ALI BABA AND HIS DOG, DELANCEY, SOLVE ANOTHER MYSTERY FOR THE POLICE. He smiled to himself. That really sounded perfect.

That evening, however, Ali Baba began to have second thoughts about his choice. He would love to have a dog, but he began to worry that his parents would be less pleased. If he gave one to them, they'd have to pretend they liked it, just the way he had to pretend he liked the turtleneck sweater his grandmother had sent him for his birthday. It was itchy, and he didn't like the color, either. But his mother made him write a nice thank-you note, and he had to wear the sweater when his grandmother came to visit—even when it was too warm a day to need a sweater.

At least his grandmother meant well. She wanted him to keep warm and not catch a cold. Deep inside, Ali Baba knew he hadn't even been thinking about his parents when he decided to get them a dog for their anniversary. If he was honest, he would have to admit that the dog would not have been a present for his parents at all. He would really have been buying it for himself. He knew that wasn't a responsible way to act. It was selfish. It would be the best present in the world for him, but not for them.

Disappointed and disgusted, Ali Baba set off along Broadway again the next day after school. He looked in the windows of all the shops he passed. There was a store selling compact discs. His parents liked music. Maybe he should buy them something in this store. Next door, there was a florist. He thought about buying flowers or a plant. There was a sale on jade plants. Ali Baba wondered if there were ivory plants.

Ali Baba crossed the street and came to the thrift shop. It was a store that sold used clothing and household items that had belonged to other people. Once his mother had bought a cake plate that she had seen in the window. Dishes didn't exactly interest Ali Baba. It was the food on them that he cared about. But he remembered that his mother had been particularly delighted with the dish. It had some fancy name and had been made in England.

Maybe here he could find something that was white, something that would be a good gift.

Inside the store, there were racks of clothing, shelves with old shoes and old books, pots and pans, and odds and ends. Ali Baba walked over to one of the shelves to see if he could find anything that looked interesting. Perhaps there was another fancy dish for his mother. Unfortunately, nothing that he saw appealed to him.

Suddenly, something on the bottom shelf caught his eye. It was a small wooden box the color of milk chocolate. Ali Baba picked it up to look at it. He was curious about what would be inside. When he opened the box, he was disappointed to discover that there was nothing in it.

"Are you interested in that box?" asked the woman who was working in the store.

"It's empty," complained Ali Baba.

"It's to put things in. Jewelry or handkerchiefs, things like that."

Ali Baba looked at the box more closely. He rubbed his hand over the top. It was very, very smooth. He could see where pieces of the wood had been attached together, but his fingers could not feel any unevenness where the parts met. He could not see any nail holes. He lifted the box and sniffed at it. There was a faint wood smell. Then Ali Baba rubbed the box against his cheek. It felt cool and pleasant. All the items in the store had formerly belonged to other people. Ali Baba wondered who had owned this wooden box, and he wondered what wonderful things had once been stored inside.

"Is this very expensive?" he asked the saleswoman.

She took the box from Ali Baba and turned it upside down. Pulling a little paper sticker off the box, she said, "I can let you have it for ten dollars. That's a very good price for this."

Ali Baba didn't know if it was a good price or not for an empty wooden box. He knew he had enough money at home, and he just knew his mother would like the box. But an anniversary gift should be for both his parents, not just one.

Then Ali Baba had an idea. He asked the woman to save the box for him while he got his money. He ran all the way home and back. Even though the woman had promised that she wouldn't sell it to anyone else, Ali Baba was afraid it might be gone by the time he returned to the shop.

The box was waiting for him under the counter, and Ali Baba paid for it. The saleswoman took his money and put the box in a paper bag. He made one more stop on his way home. Now he could hardly wait for his parents' anniversary.

"What in the world is this?" asked Mrs. Bernstein when Ali Baba presented his parents with the gift on the morning of their anniversary.

"Why, this is beautiful," she exclaimed as she pulled the wooden box out of the paper bag.

"The box is for you, and there's something inside it for Dad," said Ali Baba.

Mrs. Bernstein handed the wooden box to her husband to open. Inside, he found a cardboard box filled with white chocolates.

"They're white because this is your ivory anniversary," Ali Baba explained. "I hope you don't mind that the box isn't white."

"It's chocolate-colored," said Mrs. Bernstein.

"That's what I thought, too," said Ali Baba.

"There's going to be another chocolate-colored surprise this afternoon," Mr. Bernstein announced to his son as he left for work. "I've been planning it for a few weeks, and today is the day I'm supposed to pick it up."

Mrs. Bernstein smiled at her husband. It was obvious to Ali Baba that she knew something about this chocolate-colored surprise already.

Ali Baba tried to guess what his father was going to bring home. Chocolate-covered peanuts, chocolate-covered raisins, chocolate-covered almonds, a chocolate cake . . . Ali Baba licked his lips in anticipation.

Mr. Bernstein brought a large box home with him that evening. The box seemed to be making noises. But when he opened it, Ali Baba discovered that the box was silent. It was the contents of the box that made the noise. The noise was made by a small brown dog.

"Is that for your anniversary?" he gasped.

"It's for the whole family, but mostly it will be your responsibility."

"We could call him Chocolate," suggested Mr. Bernstein.

"Yes, we could," said Ali Baba. "But do we have to?" He was down on the floor, hugging

this newest member of the family. "I don't understand why so many people name their pets after foods. Natalie Gomez has a white cat named Marshmallow, and she knows a girl named DeDe who has a dog named Cookie."

"What would you like to name him?" asked Mr. Bernstein.

"Delancey," said Ali Baba.

"Delancey?"

"It sounds important," said Ali Baba.

"It won't make me hungry," said Mrs. Bernstein. "If we called him Chocolate, it would make me want to eat candy all the time."

"Then Delancey it is," said Mr. Bernstein.

So it was that on the day he was ten years, five months, and six days old, Ali Baba acquired a dog. It wasn't his birthday and it wasn't his anniversary, but it was the day his parents decided that he was getting responsible. They had given him the best present in the world. Now, with his new pet, he was going to prove to them that they hadn't made a mistake.

Ali Baba took the leash that his father gave him and attached it to the dog's collar. He was going to take Delancey for a walk. Who knew what adventure was waiting for them outside?